ROSES

FROM THE PAST

ROSES
FROM THE PAST

SILVIA ALVAREZ

AuthorHouse™
1663 Liberty Drive
Bloomington, IN 47403
www.authorhouse.com
Phone: 1-800-839-8640

Published by AuthorHouse   03/25/2013

ISBN: 978-1-4817-3107-2 (sc)
ISBN: 978-1-4817-3106-5 (e)

Library of Congress Control Number: 2013905058

Any people depicted in stock imagery provided by Thinkstock are models, and such images are being used for illustrative purposes only.
Certain stock imagery © Thinkstock.

This book is printed on acid-free paper.

Because of the dynamic nature of the Internet, any web addresses or links contained in this book may have changed since publication and may no longer be valid. The views expressed in this work are solely those of the author and do not necessarily reflect the views of the publisher, and the publisher hereby disclaims any responsibility for them.

This book is dedicated to my mother Silvia Haydee Alvarez (1939 to 2011), my brothers Gus Sr. and Jorge Sr. and my sister Tere also to my sisters-in-law Maria and Suzy.

But specially to my nieces and nephews; Samantha, Angela, Genevieve, Gustavo Jr., Jorge Jr. and Luie.

Contents

Roses white as snow,
That bleed, the blood of life
Tell me of the tragedy,
The trouble and the strife.

Tell of the fight
That cost a man his life,
Tell of the end,
That gave the other a wife.

Roses red as rubies,
That burn in flames of blue
Tell me of the past,
Of a love that once was true.

Tell me why they married,
Why they loved and why they fled,
Tell me now their story,
And if, they're still wed.

PROLOGUE

The wind outside of the little cottage howled and the rain beat upon the tightly closed shutters like a million tiny fists.

Inside, lying on the big double bed, cradling her two hour old twin sons, was Lady Dumas de Ramsie.

"You look radiant my love," James said to his wife as he gently kissed her forehead.

"I'm exhausted. James, please put the boys in their cribs and bring me some water," she said with a smile.

"Your wish is my command," James replied with an extravagant bow.

He put the twins to bed and left the room to go and get the glass of water that his wife had asked for.

Without thinking Mairely removed the Santa Rosalina's medallion from around her neck and placed it on the night stand beside the bed.

The yellow orange flame of the candle that sat on the night stand flickered as a gust of wind flung the shutters open and a shadowy figure begins to materialize beside Mairely's bed.

"This night I shall make you mine," said a heavy Italian accented voice.

Mairely's eyes opened wide in horror and her heart began to beat so fast that she could actually feel it against her chest.

James walked in with the glass of water just as the ghost leaned over to place a kiss on Mairely's forehead.

"Be gone spawn of Satan!" James cries as he picked up the medallion and shoved it into the specters face.

The specter growled at him and disappeared with the wind.

"Are you all right my love?" James asked as he sat down next to his wife.

"I'm just tired, that's all," she took a *deep* breath and sighed, "James, promise me that you'll take good care of the boys if anything should happen to me," she said in a small tired sounding voice.

"I promise, but I know that nothing bad will happen to you," he said as he fixed the covers around her.

"Also pray that a female is never born to those who follow, for the day that one is born, *he,* will go looking for her," she said as she throws the coverlet to one side and James takes her into his arms.

"I will my love," he said and gently kissed her lips.

"I am so very tired, I must sleep," she whispered and closed her eyes.

Mairely Cristina Dumas de Ramsie closed her eyes and fell into an eternal sleep.

James said a small prayer foe her then wept for the loss of the woman he so dearly loved.

"One day, *you* and I will come face to face and on that day I shall make sure that you will forever burn in the fires of hell," James said aloud to the darkness that surrounded him.

1970

At seven twenty-two am in a hospital in Miami Florida, the first girl was born into the Ramsie family.

Chapter I

Monday October 25, 1995

The scream in the middle of the night brought Mr. and Mrs. Ramsie running to their daughter's room.

"Sh-sh-sh, everything's all right," soothed her mother as she held her daughter close.

"Oh mom, it was horrible, I was at work and the lights go out, the all of a sudden some guy jumps me; but the strangest part about the dream is that only Jess and I were there," she cried into her mother's shoulder.

Six blocks away the same thing was happening at the Quintero home.

The scream that awakened the sleeping house brought Mr. Quintero to his son's bedside.

"Jess, are you okay?" he asked as his son sat up in his bed.

"Yeah, I'm okay now, but that dream scared the hell out of me," he said as he rubbed his forehead head with his finger tips.

"What you were having, bro, was a no dream, it was a nightmare," his younger brother said from the door way.

"Pop, why don't you go back to bed, Luie will sit with me for a while," he added as he motioned his brother into his room.

"Okay, I'll see you in the morning son," Mr. Quintero said as he made his way back to his room.

"Tell me about your nightmare," Luie said as he sat on the side of the bed.

"Okay, it was just me and Mairely at the warehouse; everything was normal then all of a sudden the lights go out, as I turn to go to Mairely's side I see someone grab her by the waist. I don't know who *he* was or where *he* came from all I know is that *his* eyes were redder than blood and had the strength of a thousand men 'cause he picked me up over his head with one hand and threw me. The last thing I remember was yelling at May, telling her to run. Then I screamed and woke up," he said and reached for the glass of water that sat on the nightstand.

"What a way to start a Monday," Luie said with a smile.

Later on that morning after Jess finished shaving and dressing he returned to his room to find a dozen bleeding white roses in the middle of his bed. He closed his eyes tight to the sight and counted to ten, when he reopened them the roses were gone.

That afternoon while at work the lights go out, when they come back on Mairely finds a red rose on her desk with a message on her computer that read: 'You will soon be eternally mine.' And Jess found a white rose on his. As he reached for the rose it began to bleed, the blood flowed from the flower onto his desk and to the floor making a small puddle by his feet.

Mairely's first thought was that Jess had put the flower on her desk and the message on her computer but when she reached for the one single rose it became surrounded by a bright blue flame, this caused her to scream.

Upon hearing the scream Jess turned towards her and saw that Ozzie, one of Mairely's closest friends, had gone to her side, when he turned back to his desk the white rose and the blood was gone.

Mairely was still shaking when Jess walked up to her and took her in his arms.

"Everything's all right now May," he said as he gently brushed a few strands of loose hair from her face. "See, there's nothing there," he added as he turned with her to show her the empty desk.

"But it was there Jess; a single red rose and it was surrounded by a blue flame but it wasn't burning and there was a message on my computer screen," she complained as she let herself be drawn back into his strong arms.

As Jess drove Mairely home from work that night she brought up the subject of what had happened at the warehouse that afternoon.

"It wasn't a red rose, May, it was a white one," he said as he gently caressed her hand.

"I'm not blind, I know what I saw, it was a red rose surrounded by a blue flame," she said and moved her hand away from his reach.

"Well I saw a white one that was bleeding and the blood was redder than my sweater," he said as the car came to a stop in front of her house. "Let's not worry about it, it's probably a coincidence any way," he add as he walked her to her door and kissed her good night.

Again that night Mairely and Jess share the same dream and wake at the same time.

Ozzie Romero, Mairely's closest friend, drove up northwest twenty-Fifth Street towards one hundred and seventh avenue when all of a sudden his car goes out of control.

SILVIA ALVAREZ

He struggles frantically with the wheel in an attempt to regain control but he realized that it was useless. He thought of jumping but the car was going too fast, so he prayed silently that it would go into the canal that way he would be able to swim to safety. But as luck would have it, the small car veered towards the closed warehouses on the other side of the street.

In a state of desperation Ozzie tried to open the door to jump but the door refused to open.

Suddenly he hears his name called. Thinking that there is someone in the back seat of the car, he looks into the rear view mirror and sees a young man sitting there, he was dressed all in black, his hair was as dark as the midnight sky and his eyes were a dark steel gray. Their eyes locked for what seemed an eternity.

"Your love for her is a threat to me," the young man said and smiled. "But soon, very soon you will cease to be a threat," he added and disappeared.

Ozzie shifted his sight just in time to see the front end of his car go smashing into the side of one of the buildings. His body lurched forward causing him to hit his head on the steering wheel and rendering him unconscious, seconds later, as if by commands of the elements, the small brown Mustang burst into flames and a low menacing laugh rang above the roaring fire.

CHAPTER II

TUESDAY OCTOBER 26

The next morning sat at home watching T.V. when all of a sudden the set goes off. He got up and checked the light s in the family room and living room, they were working fine. When he re-entered the family room he saw that the floor was completely covered by a misty white cloud of smoke. He heard his name called and he looked towards the double glass doors that lead to the patio, there, in front, of the doors he saw the figure of a young woman begin to appear.

"Jesus Quintero, I am here to warn you and all close to the one you love. You are all in danger of death.

Cross not the path of Dante de Palermo on the on the Sabbath night, for if you do you shall die and your soul will roam the earth for all eternity," the beautiful specter said in a whisper.

"Who are you and why are we in danger?" Jess asked as he stepped down into the cloud of white.

"My name is one with hers, and the answers you seek are to be found in the first letters of the family in question," she replied and disappeared along with the mist on the floor.

Jess stood absolutely still unable to believe what had just happened. He knew that Mairely had classes that morning so he went to pay Mrs. Ramsie a visit.

Jess knocked at the familiar front door and Claire Ramsie answered it.

"Jess, what a surprise, May isn't here she has a class this morning," she said as she let him in.

"Yeah, I know, I came to see you Mrs. Ramsie, there are some things I'd like to talk to you about," he said as he followed her inside.

"Please, have a seat and tell me what it is that is worrying you so much," she said as she gestured towards the sofa as she sat in the arm chair opposite him.

Jess told her of the reoccurring night mares and found out that Mairely had been having them too.

"Now I would like to tell you what happened to me just an hour ago," he said as he accepted the can of soda from her.

"Okay, tell me what happened," she smiled and sat back down.

"An hour ago I was visited by a very beautiful and I think a very dead young woman," he said as he scooted to the edge of the sofa.

"Oh come now Jess, really," Claire said with a smile.

"She had soft snow white skin, cascading brownish blonde hair and the most beautiful haunting hazel eyes that I've ever seen," at the end of his description of the woman, Claire Ramsie's face was chalk white. "Mrs. Ramsie, are you all right?" he asked as he put a hand on her shoulder.

"Yes, I'm fine. Please go on," she replied a little shaky.

Jess told her what had transpired between him and the ghostly woman.

"The only thing that has me confused is the answer that she gave me when I asked who she was and why we were in danger," he said as he sat back once again.

"Well, to begin with, you're right, the woman you saw was a ghost, her name was Mairely Cristina Dumas, that's what she meant by 'My name is one with hers,' and 'The first letters of the family in question' would be the journals that the late James Ramsie kept," she replied with a triumphant smile.

"Great, but who was she and who, in heavens name was James Ramsie!" roared Jess as he got up and began to pace around the family room.

"First of all please sit back down," Claire said calmly. "And second, please call me Claire."

"Fine," he replied as he sat back down on the sofa and took a deep to calm his nerves.

He ran his fingers through his hair and looked directly at Claire. "Who were these people," he said as his light brown eyes shone dark with worry and fear.

Claire listened as she took in every detail of his face and body.

The worry lines on his forehead and around his eyes made him look older than what he actually was, and the well defined muscles in his arms twitched from the state of anger he was in.

"Mairely Cristina Dumas was May's great-great-great grandmother and James Ramsie was her great-great-great grandfather," Claire said as she got up to get a drink for herself.

"All right, where can I get his journals?" Jess asked as he sat forwards once again.

"Let me make a phone call later and I'll call you tonight with the information. For now go home and try and get some sleep," she said as she walked him to the door.

Jess went home and stretched out on the sofa in the family room but when he closed his eyes the only thing he saw was his reoccurring dream.

Later that afternoon Claire telephoned William Ramsie, her husband's middle brother who was the family historian.

The phone of the house that sat on the corner of ninety-seventh court and twenty-Fifth Street rang and a man somewhere in his mid to late fifties answered it.

"Hi Bill, its Claire," said the voice at the other end of the phone.

"Claire, it's nice to hear from you. How's Eric? Is he treating you well?" he asked a smile in his voice.

"Yes Bill, he's treating me like a queen," she joked back. "I called because I have a favor to ask of you."

"Ask away, anything to help my favorite sister-in-law," he replied in a light tone.

"May and her boyfriend are having some crazy dreams that seem to be connected to the old family. The funny thing is that Jess, her boyfriend, knows nothing about then but he described Mairely Dumas down to a tee for me this morning.

I know that you're the family historian and you have James' old journals, would it be possible for Jess to see them?" she asked all the while hoping that he would say yes.

"Sure, anything to help them out. I won't be home tomorrow so have him come by Thursday morning," he replied in the same light tone.

"Thanks Bill, you're a doll, I'll see you Friday. Bye," she said and hung up.

William Ramsie hung the phone up and turned to go back into his study but instead he came face to face with Mairely Cristina Dumas de Ramsie.

"Help them William, for they are in grave danger," she whispered softly.

Before he was able to say anything her image disappeared.

The phone at the Quintero home rang and Jess got up and answered it.

"Hello?" he said into the receiver.

"Hi, did you get any sleep?" Claire asked.

"You're joking right, every time I closed my eyes I saw that thing attack May," he replied as he sat down.

"At least you tried. Listen, I talked to Eric's brother, William, who happens to be the family historian, he has James' old journals. He said to go by his house on Thursday and you could take a look at them," she said as she looked at her address book.

"Great, tell me where to go," he said as he took a pencil and paper from the shelf above the phone. "Thanks Claire, you're the best. Oh, one more favor, May's been wanting to go to that new Disco, Venus, and I told her that I'd take tonight, so when you see her later please tell her that I'll pick her up at ten," he said as he put the paper with the address into his wallet.

"No problem," Claire replied and hung up.

The music blared and the lights flashed as Jess and Mairely walked into the club.

The motif was outer space so the large room was decorated with various objects that one might fine floating in space.

Jess smiled, looked around and moved slightly to the beat of the music but Mairely stared terrified at the middle of the dance floor, for there stood the man that haunted her dreams. She saw no one but him and heard nothing but his voice.

"Soon my beloved, with the help of the Prince of Darkness, you will become my eternal bride," he said in a heavy Italian accented voice as he moved towards her.

Mairely screamed and fainted into Jess' arms.

When she awakened she found herself back in the car. She told Jess what she had seen and heard and Jess took her into his arms and held her tightly.

Chapter III

Wednesday October 27

As Jess left work on Wednesday afternoon he and Mairely met in the parking lot.

"I hate it when we work different shifts," Mairely said as the hugged.

"So do I," he kissed her then added. "Get going or you'll be late."

"Promise to call me later," she said as she walked backwards towards the double glass doors.

"Yes, now get," he replied with a smile.

She smiled and blew him a kiss the she turned and ran the rest of the way to the warehouse.

Later that night as Mairely walked down the hall towards the cafeteria she heard someone call her name repeatedly and sensed a faint smell of roses but the closer she got to the cafeteria the stronger the smell became stronger.

She wanted to turn and run but some strange force kept drawing her forward.

When she walked into the cafeteria her eyes grew wide with terror for there were hundreds of red roses all of which were surrounded by blue flames. She suppressed the urge to scream and closed her eyes, when she reopened them the roses were gone but in their place stood the man that haunted her dreams.

He was dressed in eighteenth century clothe, his hair was as black as a starless sky, his skin was a deathly white and he had emotionless steel gray eyes which locked with hers. He extended a hand and smiled, he moved towards her slowly. She took two steps forwards and stopped, suddenly the temperature in the room dropped drastically and she felt the evil that emanated from the man before her, the sudden change made her scream.

Two employees ran in as a result of the scream, she turned, pushed her way between them and ran back to the phone room.

"Hey, May, put your ears on, I've got Jess on the phone for you," said Miriam.

"Thanks Miriam," she said as she put on her ear phones and pushed the blinking button. "Hi," she added.

"Hey, you sound out of breath, what's wrong?" Jess asked as she came on the phone.

"I just saw that guy again, I think I'm going crazy," she said as she caught her breath.

"Calm down, you're not going crazy, what you saw is all in your mind," he said in a calm and soothing voice.

"Jess, I know what I saw," she said in an exasperated tone.

"Where'd you see him?" he asked.

"In the cafeteria," she replied.

"Did you go by yourself?" he asked calmly.

"Yes, I was by myself, so what," she was beginning to get irritated by his questions.

"What were you thinking about?" he asked ignoring her tone of voice.

"Jess, I'm not a fool and I'm not blind, I know what I saw," she complained.

"I never said you were a fool nor did I say you were blind, now please answer my question," he said calmly.

"Fine, I was thinking of that dammed demon that haunts my dreams," she said quietly.

"There, I rest my case, you were alone and thinking about that thing, so your subconscious mind let you see it, that's all," he said in a low baritone voice that made her giggle.

"Are you sure doctor?" she asked with a smile.

"Yes Madame, I am sure," he joked back. "I love May."

"I love you too Jess," she replied and they hung up.

That night everyone left in a hurry and Miriam found that she had to walk to her car alone.

The night closed in around her making her feel afraid of any small noise she heard so she hurried towards her waiting car as fast as she could.

"Just a few more seconds and I'll be safe inside my car," she said out loud to reassure herself.

She spoke to soon for out of the shadows stepped a tall, dark haired young man.

Miriam's sea green eyes locked with his which were as cold and hard as steel girders.

Miriam was unable to move and the young man kept moving towards her.

"You, my sweet, are a rare beauty among women, but alas you protect the fair Lady Ramsie, who should be my bride. If it were not for that I would make you mine," said the young man in a heavy accented Italian voice.

She tried to avoid his out stretched hand but it was impossible for she was unable to move. The young man let out a low rumbling laugh that hung vividly in the moist night air.

"Do not fight me. It is of no use to you. Your fate was sealed when you became one of *her* protectors," he said as he gently caressed her face. His hand came to rest on her slightly tanned neck.

"Fire is not for you, for your beauty would be destroyed," he added as grip tightened around her neck and was lifted off of the ground with the one hand.

Miriam struggled for breath and life but it was useless for within seconds her body was still and lifeless.

Seconds later a deep dark humorless laugh is heard but the only thing around is Miriam's lifeless body lying on the cold hard pavement, of the warehouse's parking lot.

Chapter IV

Thursday October 28

Early the next morning Jess knocked at the door of the house he was sent to, it was answered by a middle-aged man.

"Hi, my name's Jess Quintero, I was sent by Claire Ramsie," he said as he extended his hand.

"Welcome Jess, I've been expecting you," William replied as he took the offered hand and gently pulled him into the house. "Claire has told me what's been happening to you and Mairely; I certainly hope that you find your answers in James' old journals."

"I hope so too, Mr. Ramsie, I hope so too," Jess said as he followed William into a shelf lined room.

As Jess began to read the old journals he was transported back to a time of chivalry and cunning adventures.

The Italian moon gave the night an air of romance, as he walked out onto the terrace that looked out over the garden and that's when he saw her. She sat in the garden among the roses, the moon shone through her soft brown hair and in her delicate hand she held a ruby red rose.

"Beautiful night isn't James," Dante said as he walked up to his friend.

"Dante, you startled me," James said as he turned to face his childhood friend.

"What are you doing out here when the party is in there," Dante said as he nodded towards the French doors behind him.

"Admiring the garden and that exquisite creature sitting among the roses," James replied as he turned towards the view before him.

"She is beautiful is she not," Dante paused as he looked at the young woman that sat by the roses. "Come James, I shall introduce her to you," He said as he moved quickly down the terrace steps.

"My love, I would like you to meet my childhood friend James Ramsie," he said as he walked up to her.

"James, my bride to be, the fair Mairely Cristina Dumas," Dante said to James with a smile.

"An honor to meet you My Lady," James said as he took her hand with a slight bow.

"Why Lord Ramsie, the honor is mine," she replied as she looked deep into his eyes.

"When is the happy occasion?" James asked without taking his eyes from hers.

Jess stopped reading and was reeled back to the present.

"They were friends, Ramsie and Palermo were friends," he said out loud as he closed the book and picked up another marked April. He began to read and once again was transported back in time.

"James, we must stop meeting here, Dante is bound to find out," Mairely said as she looked behind her for the tenth time.

"It does not matter to me, my love, in fact I think it better if he knew that you loved me and not him," James replied taking her hands in his.

"James please, Dante and I are to be married next month," she said as she took her hands back and tried to turn away from him.

"How can you marry a man that you do not love," he gently turned her back to face him. "Do you not know that every time I see you, you take a little more of my heart? I love you Mairely, now and forever, and weather you marry me or not I will send you a dozen of the red roses that you love so much, every week for the rest of my life," he said and kissed her gently.

"Oh James, I love you too; I would tell Dante but I am so afraid of him," she said taking comfort in his arms.

"Afraid of him, why?" he asked as he moved back just enough to see her eyes.

"He vowed that he would kill anyone who tried to separate us," she replied in a whispered.

"I do not fear him and if you are the prize then I welcome his challenge. You know that I am a better swordsman than he. You must tell him Mairely," James said with determination in his voice.

"Very well I shall tell him," she said

"When?" he asked

"Soon, I promise," she said as he folded her back into his arms and kissed her.

Later that evening James rode out to the Palermo Estate.

"Lord Ramsie is here to see you sir," after announcing him the servant turned and left.

Then and only then, did Dante turn to face his visitor.

James was taken aback by the expression on Dante's face; the grey eyes that were normally warm and soft were now hard and cold as steel. His jaw was set so hard that the muscles on the sides of his neck jumped and throbbed with every breath he took.

"You, you call yourself my friend and you go behind my back and take what is rightfully mine. You, are no friend of mine, you are a low good-for-nothing snake in the grass," roared Dante as he walked towards James.

"Dante, your marriage was not meant to be, she loves me and I am prepared to fight for her love," James in an even tempered voice.

"Yes we shall fight and you will die with my blade through your heart!" Dante replied as his voice and his anger escalated with every word and his eyes now shining with the anticipation of the fight.

"When and where?" asked James as he put his hand on the hilt of his sword.

"May sixth, the day before the wedding, Monte Pellegrino at dawn, your dead body shall be my wedding present to Mairely," replied Dante with a cruel smile on his lips and his eyes shining bright with the thought of death.

"Very well but it shall be the other way around, you shall be the one to die not I," James said then turned and walked out.

Again Jess stopped reading, he closed the book and his eyes, seconds later he opens his eyes and picks up yet another book this one is marked May.

The afternoon was hot and humid and James sat in the parlor of the Dumas home.

"James, you are crazy if you go through with that stupid duel!" Mairely exclaimed as fear appeared in her eyes.

"No, I am not crazy. I cannot let him marry you. Besides, the match is all ready set and no one is going to stop me," James said in a determined voice

"James, I love you, I want you alive not dead. Please stop the duel, we will run away together but please, I beg you stop the duel," Mairely said in desperation.

"Very well, I will do my best to stop the fight but if I do not succeed you need not worry for de' Palermo will die under by blade," he replied as he took her into his arms and kissed her passionately.

"Mr. Ramsie!" exclaimed Danrick Dumas from the opened doors of the parlor. "I told you never to come here again, leave now and I shall not press charges against you," he said and turned slightly to face his daughter. "And you go to your room and do not return down stairs until I call for you."

The next morning James rode once again to the Palermo estate.

"I have come to ask that we forfeit this duel for Mairely's sake," said James standing on the steps that lead to the front door.

"You bastard!" roared Dante as he threw a punch that caught James off guard. This caused him to lose his balance and topple down the few steps behind him. "You are no longer welcomed here, not now, not ever. And if you think that I am going to pass up the opportunity to kill you, you are sadly mistaken!" roared Dante as he looked down at the still startled James.

"No Dante," James said calmly as he got up. "You are wrong, you will be the one to die, not I," he got on his horse and rode away.

On the dawn of May sixth, Dante Damiano de' Palermo, James Christopher Ramsie and the grounds of Monte Pellegrino were bathed in the red orange light of the waking sun.

De' Palermo and Ramsie draw their swords and salute each other.

The area's animals leave their lairs and hiding places to watch the fight as the sound of clashing steel filled the morning air.

Again and again their swords met in angry battle each waiting for the other to tire so that he might take the final plunge.

James' more agile body ducked, dodged and sidestepped Dante's sword, Dante, was five years James' senior so he tired quicker.

Dante saw James lower his guard for just a second and swung his sword, a quick swing and thrust, he connected with James' left arm cutting through the silk shirt and the skin beneath turning the white to crimson.

Dante stumbled on an up grown root and let his guard down, James took the opportunity and plunged his blade deep into his chest with an upwards twist.

"You have won for now . . . but . . . I . . . shall . . . return . . . to . . . claim . . . her," were de' Palermo's last words.

"You shall never have her and you shall never harm her nor her descendants for she and all who follow shall be protected by Santa Rosalina and those who love her shall be protected by a silver crucifix," James said over the dead body of Dante Damiano de' Palermo.

Later that afternoon after cleaning up, he goes to see Mairely. He tells her about the fight and about his plans to return to America with her.

On the morning of May seventh James' first stop is at the best jewelry store in town.

"Good morning sir, may I be of some help?" the young man behind the counter asked.

"Yes, I am looking for a medium sized Santa Rosalina medallion and a silver crucifix of the same size," James replied as he walked to where the young man was.

"Something like this," the young man said as he showed him the items he had requested.

James liked what he saw so he paid for the items left the shop and walked to the docks that were just a few blocks down the street to make travel plans.

Once there he learned that there were no ships sailing to America until the following month so he made arrangements to sail to England to stay with his aunt and uncle for a while.

Once again Jess stopped reading rubbed his eyes and picked up another book marked August.

"Mairely, Mairely!" James called out as he closed the front door.

"I'm up stairs, I'll be down in a moment," she replied from the upstairs bedroom.

A moment she was sitting next to her husband dressed in an elegant bathrobe.

"I've made reservations at La Maison for dinner and we were invited to the Queens Ball tonight," he said with a smile as he put his arm around her shoulder.

"James you're wonderful," she said as she hugged him tight.

"Wait the best is still to come," he said as he returned her hug.

She smiled and sat back. "You mean there's more."

"Yes, I got some time off from the office . . ."

"How much time James?" she interrupted.

"Until you give birth," he replied

"James that's too much."

"Don't worry, they understand. I also wired my aunt and uncle and made arrangements with them so that we could stay at the cottage by the lake until you give birth," he said as he helped her up.

"You are the most wonderful husband a girl could ask for," she kissed him and headed back up stairs to finish dressing.

Elegant carriages filled the cobble stone streets as they headed towards the Palace and the Queens Ball.

When they arrived they were lead to the main ballroom by a powered wigged middle aged man, there couples danced to the soft enchanting music of a waltz and others talked and laughed in groups.

The room was lavishly decorated and the various chairs and couches were upholstered in plush crimson velvet. James smiled and greeted the people that he knew, commenting on the music, the fashion and politics but Mairely just stared at the center of the dance floor, for there, dressed as they had buried him, stood Dante Damiano de' Palermo.

She saw no one but him and heard nothing but his voice.

"Soon my beloved, with the help of the Prince of Darkness, you shall become my eternal bride," he said in his heavy Italian accented voice.

She screamed and fainted into her husband's arms. When she awoke she found herself back in her room and James sitting beside her. She told him what she had seen and what she had heard in the ballroom.

"I knew he would come back but I didn't think that he'd come back this soon," he paused kissed her forehead and went on. "As long as you wear the medallion that I gave you can't harm you, so whatever you do don't ever take it off May, never," he said as he took her into his arms and held her tightly.

A month later James and Mairely are finally going to America, it was late afternoon and they awaited the carriage that would take them to the docks when a sudden gust of wind blew open the French doors that lead to the garden and before them stood Dante de' Palermo. Instantly James took Mairely into his arms.

"Beware of me James for anyone who loves her too much will die at my hands," said the specter of Palermo as he threw a blood stained white rose at his feet.

There was a vase to Mairely's right that contained the red roses that James brought her every week, as she reached her hand out towards them they became engulfed in flames of blue, upon see the flames, Dante let out a horrid scream and disappeared from sight.

Chapter V

Late afternoon October 28th

While Jess was reading James' journals, Mairely receives a visit from a very unwanted visitor.

Mairely was aroused from her sleep by the sensation that she was being watched, when she opened her eyes there was a dark haired young man standing by her bedside looking down at her.

"Who are you? How did you get into my room?" she said fear in her voice as she pulled the bed covers up to her chin.

The young man did not answer but extended his hand and caressed her cheek. His touch was like a hot burning poker set against her skin. Mairely bolted from her bed confused and scared. She wanted nothing to do with the handsome stranger who stood beside her bed and smiled at her but her body kept telling her otherwise, she could feel her desire swelling up within her.

"I don't know who you are or what you're doing here but you'd better leave before I call the cops," she forced herself to say as she picked up the phone.

"My sweet, your instrument does not work," he said in a heavy accented Italian voice.

She put the phone to her ear and just as he had said it was dead, she threw it at him and it went right through him, she screamed and ran for the door unfortunately it didn't want to open.

"There is no way my love, you are destined to be mine," he said.

"Oh god please let this be a nightmare," she mumbled as she slid to the floor and huddled in a corner next to the door.

"I can feel your body burning with desire and my touch is the only thing that can help you. There is still one man in your heat that stands between us, my love, but he too will be of no danger to us," he said as he moved towards her.

"Stay away from me!" she screamed at him putting her clenched fists to her tightly closed eyes desperately trying to drive his image and the returning desires out of her body and mind.

"Very well my love but we shall meet again on the Sabbath," he threw his head back let out a hideous laugh and disappeared.

When she reopened her eyes the man that had been in her room was gone but his laugh still hung in the air.

Back at William's house, Jess had found what he had been looking for.

The door to the room where Jess sat reading opened, he turned towards just as William walked in.

"May I take these Mr. Ramsie?" asked Jess gesturing to several of James' journals that were on the desk before him.

"Sure Jess, take anything that might be of help," William replied as he put one hand in his pocket.

"Thank you Mr. Ramsie," Jess said as he picked up the journals and got up.

"Oh, I almost forgot, I want you to have these," he took his hand out of his pocket and held up two silver necklaces. "The medallion belonged to her and the crucifix belonged to James," he added as he put them into Jess' hand.

"Thank you again," Jess said as he put the silver necklace with the crucifix over his head, as he looked up he saw that William was looking at something or someone that stood behind him.

Jess turned to see what William was looking at and he once again came face to face with the ghost of Mairely Dumas.

"I will help you as best as I can Jess, but you must protect her from him and from herself, for the change has already begun. If you cannot get her to accept the medallion then she will be lost to you forever," Mairely's ghost said as she began to fade away.

"Wait! What do you mean by 'the change has all ready begun,'" he asked as he reached out as if to stop her from leaving.

There was no answer, for the ghost had already vanished.

They walked to the front door of the house in silence and William let him out.

Jess put the journals on the passenger seat and drove to Mairely's house in silence all the while thinking of what Mairely Dumas' ghost said. He pulled into his girlfriend's drive way got out of the car and walked up to the door, before he even knocked the door opens.

"Jess, my love, I was just thinking about you," Mairely said as she took him by the arm and led him into the living room. "I've missed babe," she added as she kissed him passionately.

At first he returned the kiss willingly but when he tried to break away she tightened her grip around his neck.

"What's the matter darling, don't you love me anymore?" she asked as she pinned him against the wall.

"Of, of course I love you," he replied taken totally by surprise at the change in her.

"Then kiss me, kiss me and make me yours all at the same time," she said with as smile and began to rub her body seductively against his.

Her lips met his again, she placed a small kiss on them the bit down, not too hard but enough to draw some blood, she flicked her tongue and licked the blood from his lip.

This must be the change, as the thought entered his mind her hand had travel down his body and stopped right between his legs where she gently began to caress him in an erotic way.

It took all his concentration, strength, and will power, to pull himself away from her.

"What's s'matter, sweetie, don't cha like it?" Mairely asked a slight slur in her words.

"No, I don't, and you're not the same girl that I fell in love with," he replied as he tighten his hand around the medallion that was in his pocket.

"Oh, that Mairely was boring, I prefer the new one. Don't you?" she asked as she moved towards him once again.

"No, no, I've grown to love the old one and I'm sure that she loves me too. Do you love May?" he said as he took the medallion from his pocket and held out before him.

Instantly Mairely started to back away from him.

"Yesss," she hissed. "But get that thing away from me," she added as she backed away from him.

"Why? The Mairely that I love has always wanted a Santa Rosalina medallion," he said as he kept advancing towards her.

"Pleeease, I promise to be good, just take that away from me," she wined as she sat on the couch and brought her knees up to her chin.

Jess was now only inches away from her.

"If you love me then take the necklace from my hand and put it around your neck," he said calmly as he held the offered jewelry out to her.

"No, no, I can't," she cried but her hand was all ready extended towards the shiny silver necklace.

Her emotions were all in turmoil. She held the necklace out before her and cried freely, Jess stood there wanting to take her into his arms and hold her but he knew that he couldn't.

"I love you Jess, I really do, please help me," she said in a weak voice.

"I love you too May, but you have to do this on your own," he replied holding himself back with all the strength he could summon.

Slowly, with unsteady hands she put the necklace over her head and let it fall into place, once it touched her chest she fainted.

Jess looked down at her, then sat at the edge of the couch and took her into his arms.

"M-m-m, I must've fallen asleep on the couch. How long have you been here?" she asked as she stretch and snuggled deep into the embrace.

"Not long, love, not long," he replied as he held her tightly against his chest.

He never did tell her what had occurred between them on that certain Thursday afternoon.

Chapter VI

Friday October 29TH

On Friday morning Jess went to see Claire.

"Jess, what a surprise, I was just thinking about you," Claire said as she let him into the house.

"Hi," he replied as he walked in. "Come sit with me, I have something that I want to read to you," he added as he waved James' journals in the air and sat on the couch.

"I gather you found something important," she said as she sat across from him.

"Yes, indeed I did. Listen to this," he said as he picked up the journal marked March and began to read.

"March first; every time I see her my love for her grows deeper and when I see her smile my heart melts like butter.

I have finally met her face to face but my heart has been crushed for I have learned that she is to marry my childhood friend, Dante Dominico de' Palermo, on the morning of May seventh.

March ninth; my heart is once again whole, for Mairely's private servant came to me in the early morning hours with the news that she does not love Dante, she loves me. There must be a way to stop this union," Jess stopped reading put the book down and looked a Claire.

"Don't stop now, I want to know what happens," she said in an excited voice.

"I'll read you the last few days of April," he said and picked up the journal marked April and began to read.

"April twenty-eighth; Mairely finally told her parents that she did not want to marry Dante that she loved me and would marry only me.

April twenty-ninth; Dumas Manor was in an uproar this morning, Mr. Danrick Dumas has forbidden his daughter to step outside the protective walls of the estate.

In the afternoon I went to see Dante, he yelled, screamed and denounced me as his friend. He challenged me to a duel which is to be held at dawn on May sixth.

April thirtieth; this morning I talked to Mairely and she begged me to stop the fight.

Again I rode to de' Palermo Manor and called Dante out. My visit was to be one of peace but he was insulted by my visit. His words were angry then he struck me," Jess paused and Claire looked at him unable to believe what she was hearing.

Jess picked up the third book which was marked May.

"May sixth; it is now midnight, it has been eighteen hours since I killed Dante, I am more afraid now than I was before for as he lay dying he said, and I quote, 'you have won for now but I shall return to claim what is rightfully mine,' shortly after he passed away I condemned his soul to the eternal fires of hell, then I recited a prayer to Santa Rosalina asking her to protect Mairely and all her ancestors and one to our Lord Jesus Christ to protect all those who love her.

May seventh; the first thing I did this morning was to buy her a Santa Rosalina medallion and a crucifix for myself, then I went to the docks to make travel arrangements to America but as fate would have it there were no ships leaving till the next month, so I booked passage to England to stay with an aunt that lives there. We left that same night and were married aboard ship."

Jess had still another book, this one marked August. He picked it up and began to read before Claire could interrupt him.

"Thursday August twelfth; my beloved Mairely is with child and we will be finally going to America.

Friday August thirteenth; we awaited the coach that would take us to the docks when the French doors that led to the garden blew open with a sudden gust of ice cold wind and there before us stood the ghost of Dante Dominico de' Palermo. Instantly I took Mairely into my arms.

He warned us that anyone that loved or protected her would die at his hand then he threw a blood stained white rose at our feet to make his warning clear. Mairely reached for a red rose that sat in a vase near us and instantly the whole bunch were surrounded by a blue flame.

Dante screamed horribly and disappeared. This was also a warning, he has not yet been consumed by the fires of hell do he is afraid of fire."

"I don't believe it, Dante and James were friends until Mairely fell in love with James," said Claire as she got up and began to pace the floor.

Jess watched his mother-in-law to be carefully, the soft chestnut brown hair that fell slightly past her shoulders should have been black for she was almost her daughter's mirror image.

She stopped pacing and turned to face Jess. He noticed that her normally clear blue eyes were clouded over with fear.

"I better buy May that medallion," she said as she sat on the couch next to Jess.

"You don't have to Claire," he said as he put his hand over hers.

"How can you say that, she's my daughter, I have to protect her," Claire said as a tear escaped her eyes.

"Calm down, the threats are directed to me and besides, when I was a Williams yesterday he gave me the original medallion and crucifix," he said and showed her the crucifix that now hung around his neck.

Jess left the Ramsie house with a feeling of uncertainty. He had seen fear and confusion in Claire's clear blue eyes as she had closed the door behind him.

Later that night as Claire prepared the evening meal the lights in the kitchen and family room went off.

Not sensing any danger she began to check the lights, none of them would turn on. Full of frustration she turned towards the living room, there she saw that two small table lamps were on and gave the room an eerie yellowish glow that didn't quite reach the corners of the room.

A hissing like sound emanated from the far right corner of the room and Claire turned towards it. The hissing grew louder and louder until it sounded more like a whisper instead of a hiss.

"You shall help me obtain what is rightfully mine," whispered the voice that came from the corner in a heavy Italian accent.

Claire retreated two steps as the figure of a man slowly walked out of the shadows.

Claire tried to move away from the advancing figure but found that she was frozen in place by his red eyed stare. He now stood beside her and smiled then he bent slightly, whispered something into her ear and disappeared.

Claire slumped against the bar and waited for her strength to return then slowly stood and returned to the kitchen to finish cooking.

"Mom, I'm home!" Mairely called from the front as she closed and locked it.

"I'm in the kitchen sweetie," her mother replied.

Mairely walked into the kitchen and gave her mother a hug and a kiss on the cheek.

"M-m-m, something smells good. What's for dinner?" she asked as she lifted the lid off of one of the pots.

"May I see the medallion that Jess gave you?" Claire asked ignoring her daughter's question.

"Umm, sure," May said as she revealed the medallion that was hidden by the bright violet top that she wore.

"Please take it off so that I can see it better," Claire said as she got closer to her daughter.

"No, Jess told me never to take it off," she said as she tucked it back inside her top.

"Come on May, I'm your mother, I'm not going to steal it I just want to get a real close look at it," Claire said.

Mairely noticed that her mother's voice had gone up in pitch as it normally did when she was angry or upset.

"Why are you angry with me mom?" asked Mairely as she backed away from her mother.

"I'm not angry, I'm just upset that you won't show me the medallion," she replied as she followed her daughter out of the kitchen.

"I did show it to you I just won't take it off," she said as she reached blindly for the telephone behind her.

"Who are you going to call?" her mother asked impatiently.

"Jess, he asked me to call him when I got home," she replied with the phone now held firmly in her hand.

"I don't like that boy, I never have. I really think that you should stop seeing him," said Claire as she reached for the phone in her daughter's hands.

Mairely sidestepped her and ran for her room.

"Mairely Cristina Ramsie, unlock the door this instant!" her mother yelled as she pounded at her daughter's bedroom door.

In the safety of her room she called Jess.

"Hello," he answered on the second ring.

"Jess, you have to come right now, my mom is acting strange and I'm really scared," Mairely said not giving him a chance to speak.

"Okay, calm down, I'll be there in ten minutes. In the mean time stay in your room and keep the door locked," he said in a calm voice.

He hung up and went to the kitchen for his car keys, as he turned to head back towards the front door he came face to face with a young man that looked a lot like Mairely's father.

"She is under Dante's power, you will need this to free her from him," the ghost of James Ramsie said.

As he disappeared a sterling silver necklace with a sterling silver crucifix attached to it appeared in thin air; Jess caught it before it hit the floor.

Why the crucifix he thought as he put it in his pocket, then he remembered the passage from the journal. 'All that protect her shall be protected by a silver crucifix.'

Back at the Ramsie house things were getting worse.

"I know you called him. And I know he's coming but he can't do anything, he's just a helpless little boy trying to do a man's job," her mother said as she jimmied a screwdriver between the door and the frame and pried it open. "Now give me the medallion before I get angrier that what I all ready am," she added as she walked into her daughter's bedroom.

"No, I promised Jess that I would never take it off not even for you, mom," Mairely said as she put her hand over the medallion and tried to avoid her mother.

Claire took another step towards Mairely just as the door bell rang, she hesitated and Mairely slipped past her and ran for the front door.

"Come back here young lady, we have unfinished business," Claire called after her as she followed her back towards the living room.

Mairely opened the door and ran right into Jess' arms.

"She's gone crazy, Jess, she's scaring me and I don't know what to do," Mairely cried as Jess walked into the house with her in his arms.

"I know what to do, just close the door so she can't get out," he said as he put himself between Mairely and her on coming mother.

"Ah, I see the boy has arrived" said Claire as she came face to face with Jess.

"Hello Claire," he said as he reached into his pocket and closed his hand over the necklace.

"Hello boy. I gather you think you can save her from him," she said as she tried to get to her daughter.

"I may not be able to save her from him at this moment but I can save her from you and you from him," he said as he produced the necklace with the crucifix from his pocket.

As soon as Claire saw it she stopped trying to get to Mairely and took two steps back.

"Where did you get that? Take it away it doesn't belong to me," she said as she kept moving backwards without taking her eyes off of the necklace.

"Of course it belongs to you; you had me take it to the jewelers to get repaired. Don't you remember," he said as he guided her away from the family room and the sliding glass door.

Claire didn't take her eyes away from the necklace in his hand and walked right into the couch in the living room. She looked around, no way to escape and he was almost upon her, she sat down and brought her knees up to her chest and rested her forehead on them.

"Please take it away, he'll be extremely angry if I take it from you and don't complete my mission," she said as she began to rock back and forth.

"And what is your mission?" he asked as he knelt before her.

"I am to make sure that she doesn't have the medallion on come the Sabbath for that's when *he* will come for her," Claire replied as she pointed at her daughter.

"What's she talking about Jess," Mairely asked as she watched her mother from over Jess' shoulder.

"First I have to break her trance. Then I'll explain everything with your mother's help," he said without taking his eyes off of Claire.

"Please, I beg you, tell her to take the necklace off," said Claire as tears began to run freely down her cheeks.

"I'll tell her to take off the necklace if you put this one on," he said as he held out his hand.

"Promise," said Claire as she timidly reached for the offered jewelry.

"Yes I promise but you have to put this on first," he said as her hand got closer to his.

Claire closed her hand over the necklace and brought it up to her face to get a closer look at it. When she saw the crucifix her eyes got so wide that Mairely thought that they would pop out of their sockets.

Before she could react any farther Jess took the necklace from her hand and placed it around her neck. Claire screamed as the crucifix came to rest on her chest and passed out.

Mairely rushed to her mother's side and gently patted her on the cheek.

"Mom, mom, please wake up," she urged as she sat on the edge of the couch.

"M-m-m, what, I must've fallen asleep. Oh my god, dinner, I left the stove on . . ." she was interrupted mid sentence.

"Don't worry I turned it off," Jess said as he walked back into the living room.

"Okay, my mom is fine now, so please tell me what's going on," Mairely said in a stern voice.

Claire looked at Jess and shook her head no.

"We have to Claire, it involves her more than anyone else," he said as he sat down across from them.

"Okay, the whole story in a nut shell; there's this guy, Dante de' Palermo, he was best friends with your great-great-great grandfather, James Christopher Ramsie and was to marry Mairely Cristina Dumas—your great-great-great grandmother—but she fell in love with James so Dante and James became enemies, they fought for Mairely's hand, James won, he damned Dante to hell and cursed the Ramsie blood line to only have sons, you were born, the curse was broken now Dante's back to claim his bride. You," Jess said trying to be convincing.

"Mom is what he said all true?" she asked her mother.

"Every last word, the only thing he failed to tell you is that Dante will eliminate anyone that stands in his way if they're not protected," she replied as she held up the silver crucifix.

"So the medallion should keep me safe from him," she said in a shaky voice.

"Yes it should, like the crucifix should keep me and your mom safe," he said as he took her hands in his.

"So the guy I've been seeing is this Dante?" she asked trying to get a handle on her fear.

"Yes, and all the things that we've been seeing are warnings and some are threats, like what just happened to your mom," he replied with a squeeze to her hands.

"Then as long as we wear the necklaces we're safe?" she tentatively asked.

"We're safe until Sunday, what's going to happen then I don't know," he said in a worried voice.

That night, since her father was out of town, Mairely slept with her mother.

Chapter VII

Saturday October 30th

The day was bright and cool, the perfect weather to be outdoors.

Jess and Mairely were to celebrate their third year anniversary of being together and Jess had planned a special surprise for her.

He had called a couple of their friends and had them set up a portable gazebo style tent at Tropical Park and in the middle of the tent they set out a blanket with food and wine, all ready for when they got there.

Jess dialed her number and waited.

"Hi beautiful," he said when Mairely answered the phone.

"Hi, what's up?" she asked trying to sound casual.

"What do you say we go to the park and just hang out there?" he asked as a smile crept into his voice.

"The park, to hang out, that's it?" she asked sounding disappointed.

"Yeah, it's the perfect day for it," he replied trying not to chuckle.

"Great, I'm on my way to pick you up," he said and hung up.

Please Lord, no ghosts today, he thought as he grabbed his keys and headed out of the door.

He reached her house ten minutes later.

He knocked at the door expecting Mairely to answer but her mom answered it instead.

"She'll be here in a few minutes. Listen, she had a real bad night so I hope you have something really nice for today," she said as she looked back for her daughter.

"I think so; I have a picnic lunch waiting for us at Tropical Park. You think she'll like it," he asked timidly.

"She'll love it," Claire replied with a smile.

"I'll love what?" Mairely asked as she walked up behind her mother.

"Christ you scared me!" Claire exclaimed as she turned to face her daughter.

"Sorry. What will I love?" she asked again in a mischievous tone.

"You'll see," Jess said as he reached for her hand.

As Mairely walked away her mother called out. "May, remember that I'm going to visit you Uncle William today so I may not be home when you get here."

"Okay mom, have fun and I'll see you when you get home," she yelled back as the car began to move.

The music from the radio fills the quiet car as they head for the park. Both submerged in their private thoughts.

"I have a special surprise for you but you have to wear a blind fold," he said as he helped her out of the car and showed her the blue bandana that was to be her blind fold.

She looked at him and smiled. She knew that as long as she was with him she would be safe so she turned her back to him and let him place the bandana over her eyes.

40

He took her hands and led her across the parking lot to the grassy area of the park and led her out a little farther.

"Are you ready for your surprise," he whispered into her ear causing her to giggle.

"Yes," she replied with a smile.

He took the bandana off of her eyes and she blinked a few times to adjust her sight.

"Oh Jess, this is beautiful," she said when she saw the picnic lunch spread out before her.

Her favorite flowers sat in a vase in the middle of the blanket, her favorite wine sat in an ice bucket along with the glasses and everything she like to eat sat around the flowers just waiting for them to come and enjoy themselves.

"Well I'm glad you like it," Jess said with a big smile on his face. "C'mon let's eat."

They sat and ate while they talked about their future and other things.

After a while the temperature began to drop and a strange mist appeared on the ground around them.

As they look up they see a figure of a man walking towards them.

Mairely moved closer to Jess and he put his arm around her shoulders and draws her still closer to him.

"Stop, don't come any closer," he said as he put his other hand up to stop the oncoming man.

"That's Dante isn't it," she whispered.

"Who are you?" Jess asked all ready knowing the answer to his question.

The man stopped and smiled. "You know who I am. You cannot protect her forever come tomorrow I shall claim what rightfully belongs to me," the man said in a heavy Italian accent and disappears.

Back at William's house he and Claire are sitting on the couch in the family room discussing everything that had been happening when the lights began to flicker, and the temperature drops drastically.

"Oh here we go again," William whispered to Claire.

Two ghostly figures begin to appear before them, a man that neither of them had seen before and the woman that they both knew as Mairely Cristina Dumas de Ramsie.

"We are here to warn you and the young man who loves and protects the one who bares my name," said the ghost of Mairely as she floated down to stand before them. The man followed her example and now also stood before William and Claire.

"Tomorrow he shall return, with more power than before for it is all hallows eve, the only time that we can walk among you. He will stop at nothing to reclaim what he thinks he lost. They should be ready, tell them to remember the roses," the man said as they both disappeared.

"I think I better leave, the kids will be home soon and I have to tell them about tomorrow," Claire said as she got up.

"Yes you're right," William said as he walked to the door.

Later that night as Jess, Claire and Mairely sat in the family room discussing all that had happened during the day the temperature drops and Mairely Dumas appears before them.

She looked at Mairely and smiled.

"My child, you are as beautiful as a wild rose, no wonder he wants you like he wanted me," the ghost said as she floated down to stand before them.

"Why are you here?" Claire asked no longer afraid.

"I have come with one final warning; beware the fire, you must get out before the fire starts or you shall both die," she said and faded away.

"A fire, the warehouse is going to be set on fire," Mairely said not believing her own words.

Chapter VIII

Sunday October 31ST

The darkness faded slowly but did not disappear completely. The dark gray sky threatened rain and the wind made the muggy day chilly and depressing.

By nine am Jess and Mairely were at their desks ready to start the work day.

They thought that they were ready for whatever might happen but they were wrong.

A little before noon the lights began to flicker; Mairely gets up and moves closer to Jess.

At the stroke of midday the lights go out completely.

The department managers start clear out the building, all have left but two.

As the double glass doors close Jamie Ross, one of the assistant managers locks them and stands guard before them.

"Trent, make sure that the cargo bay and the back door are locked down," Jamie said to the young man that stood before him.

"Yes sir, right away," Trent replied as he turned and ran towards the cargo bay.

As Jess and Mairely reach the front door they find Jamie standing there blocking their way.

"Jamie, please move so we can get out," Jess said as he took a step towards the door.

"Sorry Jess, if you want to leave I'll let you out but she can't leave. He'll get extremely angry at us if we let her leave," Jamie replied as he readied himself for a fight.

"Fine, I don't want to fight you," he said to Jamie. "Come on, we'll get out through the cargo bay," he add to Mairely as he took her hand and headed towards the back of the warehouse.

As they reached the cargo bay they saw that Trent stood guard by the back door. Again they had the same response; he would let Jess go but not Mairely.

"Now what do we do?" Mairely asked as tears ran down her face.

"Relax, I'll find a way out. I promise that I won't let anything happen to you," he said as he wrapped his arms around her.

Just then the hall way starts to get really cold and a mist covers the floor.

They hear a malicious laugh and when they look towards the end of the hall they see a man advancing towards them.

"You are a fool; you should have left when you had the chance now I shall have to kill you like I did the others," the man said in a heavy Italian accented voice.

"I'm not afraid of you Dante, I will protect her from you one way or another," Jess said to the specter before him as he pushed Mairely behind him.

"Very well, then you shall die and she shall become mine," Dante said and flicked a hand towards Jess.

Jess was sent flying backwards like an old rag doll the only problem was that he had taken a hold of Mairely's hand and she went with him.

Dante screamed in frustration as he saw his prize go flying away from him.

"Go, run!" Jess exclaimed as he took her hand and took off running back towards the cargo bay.

"You can run all you want but you cannot hide from me. One way or another I will make you mine tonight Mairely. We will become one just like it was suppose to be," Dante said as he entered the cargo bay.

Just as Dante cleared the cargo bay door they tried to run out but Dante reached out and caught Mairely by the arm. She screamed and tried to pull her arm free.

"Jess, help me!" she cried out as she raked the finger nails of her other hand across Dante's face. To his surprise she had left three bloody gouges across his cheek.

Jess heard her scream, when he turned he saw that Dante had grabbed her, them he saw the blood where she had racked her finger nails across his cheek.

He looked around for something he could use as a weapon and found a tire iron behind some oil drums. He picked it up and snuck up behind Dante, he lifted the tire iron and swung it hard at Dante's head; if he would have been human the hit would have killed him.

He let go of Mairely and faced Jess.

"That was not a nice thing to do," he said with a maniacal grin and drew his sword.

"He is not the one you want to fight Dante," said a voice from behind him.

Dante forgot about Jess and turned to come face to face with James Christopher Ramsie.

"I see you have also returned," Dante said as he lifted his sword.

"Yes I have. I returned to stop you once again," James replied as he drew his sword.

Jess and Mairely hid behind some oil drums and watched as the two men faced off.

Dante and James face each other swords drawn, the circle each other waiting for the other to make a move. Then without warning Dante lunges forward, James back steps and blocks his sword, Dante swings for his head and James ducks and returns the blow.

James advances upon Dante backing him up to the big cargo bay doors, Dante blocks his blows one after another. James swings and misses but his sword hit a dangling chain and cause a spark. The spark lands in an open container of oil and a small fire starts.

No one notices the fire and the fight continues.

The steel blades collide and clangs are heard every time they come together.

James bumps into one of the oil drums and it tips over causing the oil to run out and head towards the drums where Jess and Mairely were hiding. A spark from the fighting blades lands in the oil from the upturned drum and sets it on fire.

The fire starts to move quickly towards Jess and Mairely, by then the whole cargo bay is full of smoke and fire.

"C'mon May, we have to get out of here," he said as he took her hand and began to pull her along.

When they reached the door it was all ready engulfed in flames.

"We can't go through there, we'll catch fire," Mairely said as she began to cough.

"Water," Jess said and turned. "There's a water dispenser in Jerry's office. If we can reach it before the flames we can wet ourselves down and we'll have a better chance of getting out of here with minimal burns," he said still holding on to her hand.

"You will never make out that way," said a voice from behind them.

They turned and Mairely came face to face with basically herself.

"You look like me," she said and coughed.

"Actually you look like me," the ghost said and smiled. "Come I will hold back the fire so that you can escape," she said and the fire that had blocked their escape route dwindled and disappeared.

They could still hear the clash of swords as they followed the ghost of Mairely Ramsie through the halls of the burning building.

"You will never bother my family again Dante, this time you *will* burn!" James yelled over the roar of the fire.

"If I burn so shall you James and she will never see you again!" Dante yelled back.

Just then a big black hole opened on the concrete floor of the cargo bay and a dark figure appeared floating above it.

"You have eluted me for a long time now. I think it is time for you to come home," the figure said in a multitude of voices as it took hold of Dante and began to pull him through the black hole. Dante screamed as the blue flames touched his body.

As Dante was being consumed by the fires of hell Jess and Mairely crashed through the front doors out into the open followed closely by Jamie and Trent.

Someone had called the owner and the fire department but the fire had gotten out of hand and could not be contained.

"Is it over?" Mairely asked as she let Jess pull her into an embrace.

"Yeah, I think so," he replied as he placed a gentle kiss on her lips.

As they turned to leave James and Mairely appear to them one last time.

"Thank you for protecting her. May you both live in happiness forever," they said in unison and disappeared.

The End.

About the Author

My name is Silvia Alvarez and I live in Miami, Florida with my brother, his wife and their four kids. They also have four dogs and a parrot.

I am a massage therapist by trade but my first passion is the written word so I have many stories that will hopefully make it into books one day.